Enjoy this story — my grand-
children did.
Aunt Bev.

This edition published by Parragon Inc. in 2013.

Parragon Inc.
440 Park Avenue South, 13th Floor
New York, NY 10016
www.parragon.com

ISBN 978-1-4723-2715-4

Printed in China

5 Minute Bedtime Tale

The Three Little Pigs

Retold by Kath Jewitt

Illustrated by Mei Matsuoka

PaRragon

Bath • New York • Singapore • Hong Kong • Cologne • Delhi
Melbourne • Amsterdam • Johannesburg • Shenzhen

Once upon a time, there were three little pigs who lived in a cozy cottage on the hill.

They loved to eat all the delicious food their mother made them every day. They ate so much, that it wasn't long before the three little pigs had grown so big that there was no room for them in the cozy cottage any more.

"I'm sorry," said their mother one morning, "but it's time you made your own way in the world."

So the very next day, the three little pigs left home.

"Don't forget to watch out for the Big Bad Wolf," called their mother, as she waved goodbye. "He'll eat you for supper, so you'll need to build a big, fine, strong house as quickly as you can to keep him away."

"Don't worry, Ma!" they oinked. "We can look after ourselves!"

And the three little pigs trotted off down the hill, each taking a different path.

It wasn't long before the
first little pig met a farmer
pulling a cart filled
with straw.

"Please may I buy some straw to build a house?" asked
the little pig.

"Of course," replied the farmer, "but a straw house won't
be very strong!"

But the little pig didn't listen. Soon he was busy stacking the bundles of straw for his new house.

In no time at all, the house of straw was finished, and the little pig went inside for a nap.

He had just shut his eyes, when there was a knock at the door.

It was the Big Bad Wolf. And he was hungry!

"Little pig, little pig, let me in!" growled the wolf.

"No way!" cried the little pig. "Not by the hair on my chinny-chin-chin!"

"Then I'll HUFF…
and I'll PUFF… and
I'll blow your house
down!" laughed the
wolf. And that's just
what he did.

HUFF! PUFF! WHOOSH!

Meanwhile, the second little pig was
walking along the road when he saw
a woodcutter, piling up sticks.

"Please may I buy some sticks?" he asked
politely. "I want to build a house."

"Of course," answered the woodcutter, "but a
house made of sticks will soon fall down!"

But the second little pig
wasn't listening. He was
much too busy planning
his new stick home.

Soon the house was finished. The little pig had just
sat down to rest, when there was a knock at the door.

It was the Big Bad Wolf. He was even hungrier now!

"Little pig, little pig, let me in!" he growled.

"No way! Not by the hair on
my chinny-chin-chin!" cried the
second little pig.

"Then I'll HUFF… and
I'll PUFF… and I'll blow
your house down!" cried
the wolf. And that's
exactly what he did.

HUFF! PUFF! WHOOSH!

Meanwhile, the third little pig had met a builder.

"Please may I buy some of your bricks to build a house?" he asked.

"Of course," replied the builder. "A fine, strong house of bricks will last forever!"

The third little pig took the builder's advice. He would build the strongest house in the land!

Finally, after a hard day's work, the house was finished. It had four strong walls of brick, a tiled roof, a sturdy wooden door, and a large fireplace with a chimney.

The third little pig had just put a pot of turnips on the fire to boil, when he saw his brothers running down the road—closely followed by the Big Bad Wolf.

"Quick!" cried the third little pig. "Hide in here!"

The wolf, who was very hungry by now,
banged on the sturdy front door.

"Little pigs, little pigs, let me in!" he growled, his tummy rumbling very loudly with hunger.

"No way! Not by the hairs on our chinny-chin-chins!" cried the three little pigs.

"Then I'll HUFF… and I'll PUFF… and I'll blow your house down!" laughed the wolf.

So he HUFFED...

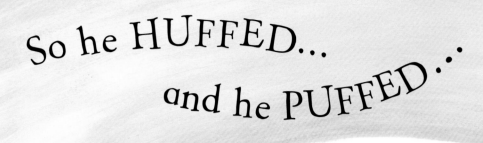

and he PUFFED...

and he PUFFED...

and he HUFFED...

But the brick house stood firm.

The wolf was furious! He climbed up onto the
roof and shouted down the chimney.

"If I can't blow your house down, I'll come
down the chimney and gobble you all up!"

The Big Bad Wolf jumped and landed with a huge
SPLASH! in the pot of turnips boiling on the fire below.

EEEEEEEYOWWWW!

He leaped up with
a scream and ran out
of the house, never to
be seen again.

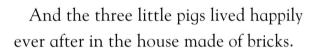

And the three little pigs lived happily
ever after in the house made of bricks.

The End